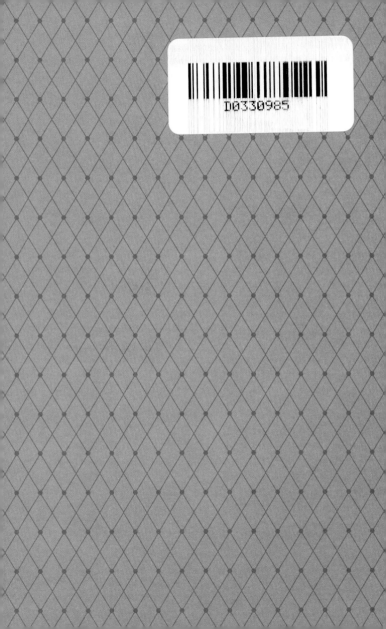

# STERLING CHILDREN'S BOOKS
New York

An Imprint of Sterling Publishing
387 Park Avenue South
New York, NY 10016

ISBN 978-1-4027-8334-0 (hardcover)

Library of Congress Cataloging-in-Publication Data Available
Distributed in Canada by Sterling Publishing
c/o Canadian Manda Group, 165 Dufferin Street
Toronto, Ontario, Canada M6K 3H6
Distributed in the United Kingdom by GMC Distribution Services
Castle Place, 166 High Street, Lewes, East Sussex, England BN7 1XU
Distributed in Australia by Capricorn Link (Australia) Pty. Ltd.
P.O. Box 704, Windsor, NSW 2756, Australia

For information about custom editions, special sales, and premium and corporate
purchases, please contact Sterling Special Sales at 800-805-5489
or specialsales@sterlingpublishing.com.

Printed in China
Lot #:
2   4   6   8   10   9   7   5   3
04/13

www.sterlingpublishing.com/kids

SILVER PENNY STORIES

# The Elves and the Shoemaker

Told by Deanna McFadden

Illustrated by Marcos Calo

Once upon a time there lived a shoemaker who worked very hard, but he was still poor. Soon the shoemaker only had enough leather left for one more pair of shoes.

The sun had set, and the weary shoemaker needed to go to bed. He cut the final bits of leather and planned to work with them first thing in the morning.

The next morning, the shoemaker was up early. The sun wasn't even out yet. After his wife made him a small breakfast, he went downstairs to make his last pair of shoes.

When he sat down at his bench he discovered that the shoes were already finished, and they were perfect in every way.

Outside, the sun was just beginning to rise.

"Who could have done this?" the shoemaker asked himself.

He had no idea. He stood up from his workbench and placed the shoes in his shop window.

Before long, a man came into the store. He liked the shoes so much that he paid handsomely for them.

The shoemaker now had enough money to make two more pairs of shoes.

Once again he carefully cut the leather. Then he went upstairs and had dinner with his wife. The next morning he came downstairs to find two new pairs of shoes on his workbench!

The shoemaker shook his head. He couldn't believe it had happened again.

Two more customers bought the well-made shoes.

He had enough money to buy leather for *four* pairs.

Every evening, the shoemaker would cut his leather. And every morning when he came down to the shop, all the shoes were made.

The shop grew successful, and the shoemaker was no longer poor. Customers filled his store from morning 'til night, buying his shoes.

The shoemaker said to his wife, "Maybe we should hide in the workshop tonight and see who has been helping us."

At midnight, two tiny little men appeared. They sat down at the workbench and nimbly made the shoes with their small fingers. They didn't stop until the leather for every last pair was used.

Morning light poked through the windows. The elves quickly finished up their work and ran away, leaving behind many pairs of beautiful shoes.

The shoemaker and his wife came out of their hiding place. The wife said, "Those elves have made us happy and wealthy. But did you see? They have nothing!"

She thought for a minute and said, "I'll make them some warm, comfortable clothes. You can make them shoes. We'll leave these presents for them on the workbench tonight."

The shoemaker agreed heartily. They were busy all day making the presents for the elves. That night, they hid downstairs and waited.

The elves crept in at midnight. At first, they didn't see the presents. They were quite confused.

"Where is the shoe leather?" they asked.

Then they saw the tiny shirts, sweet little hats, and beautiful shoes. They tried the clothing on. Everything fit wonderfully.

The elves were so pleased with the gifts that they danced and sang right out the door of the shop.

The shoemaker and his wife never saw them again. But it didn't matter. They were forever grateful for all the elves had done. The shoemaker and his wife were happy. They continued to make shoes, and their shop was celebrated throughout the land.